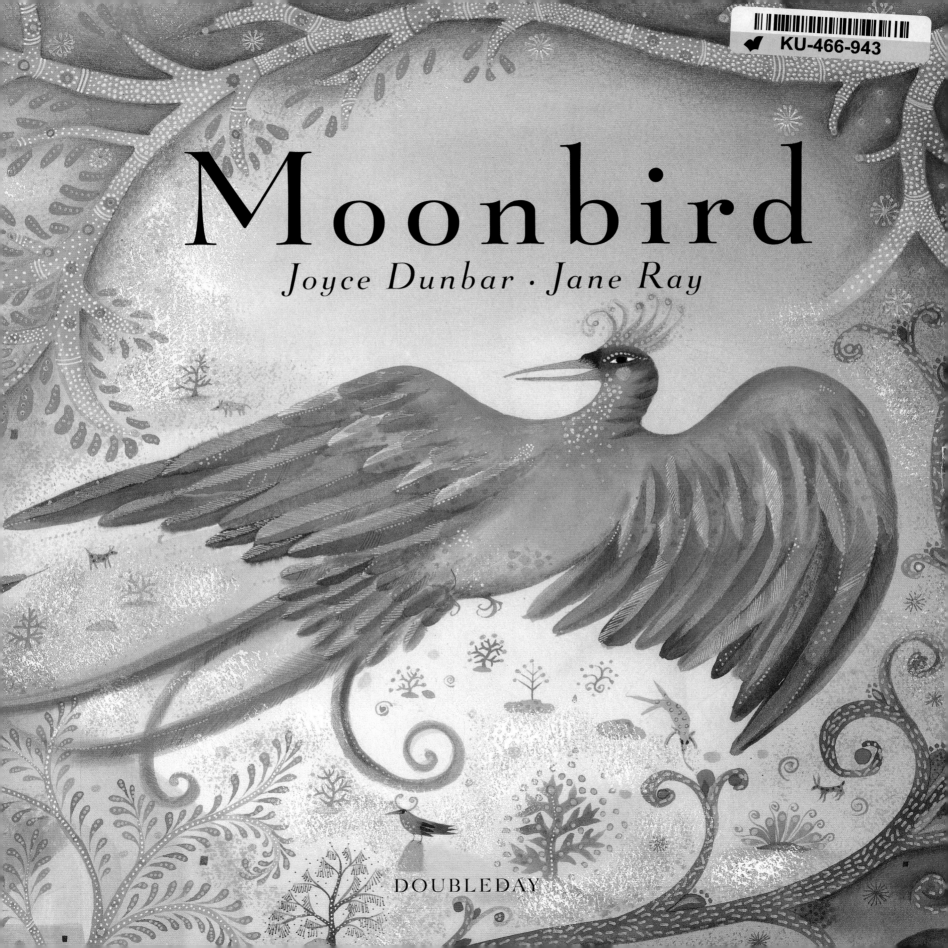

Moonbird

Joyce Dunbar · Jane Ray

DOUBLEDAY

Moonchild was blowing bubbles.

Big, pearly moon bubbles they were,

floating off into outer space.

Some burst upon the spikes of stars. Some floated all the way to earth and burst wherever they landed.

One landed
by an earth baby's ear.
"Pop!" it went, wrapping the child up
in silence. But this was no ordinary silence.
This was the silence of the moon.
"What's wrong with our child?" said the earth
baby's father, who happened to be a king.
"My baby doesn't smile when I sing," said the
earth baby's mother, who happened to be a
queen. "He doesn't listen for his name."
Louder and louder she called,

They
sent for the royal soothsayer.
She shook a silver rattle by the baby's ear.
Orla did not turn his head.
"Your child cannot hear us," said the soothsayer.

"Can't hear!" said the Queen. "You mean the royal
prince is deaf?"

"Oh no, not deaf," said the soothsayer. "This child can
hear, but not earth sounds with his ears. He hears
different sounds, in a different way."

"That can't be so," said the King and
Queen. "Of course he can
hear us."

But no matter how the King and Queen shouted, their son did not hear them.

Because
he could not hear, Orla did
not learn to speak. The King and
Queen were heartbroken. How could
their child ever be a king?

Orla became known as the silent
prince. His parents sent far and
wide for people to help him,
but nothing worked.

Until
one day, when Orla was
five years old. He was playing
in the palace gardens alone
when he spied a moonbird in a
tree. The moonbird spread his
patterned wings and spoke
to Orla.

"Follow me," said the bird.

Orla was so surprised to hear a voice that he could only do as he was told. There was magic in the moonbird's song. Whoever heard it found themselves in a moon garden, where fruit and flowers grew never seen on earth, and where animals had magical powers.

At first Orla slept in the moon garden. When he awoke, he found a soft-eyed gazelle staring into his face. Just like the moonbird, the gazelle spoke so that Orla could hear. "As I speak with my eyes, you can listen with yours," she said. "It is a gift. You will be able to share it with your mother and father."

A silver monkey helped to care for the young prince. With his hands and the movement of his body, the monkey talked to him.

Soon, Orla could talk with his hands as well as any of the young silver monkeys. They could send messages across great distances as they leaped along the treetops. They made mischief and played jokes.

With the gazelles he heard the music in the trees when the breeze blew. "Eye music," they called it. They heard voices in pools and laughter in leaves and singing in waving grass.

The moonbird appeared again. "It is time to return to your family," he said to Orla.

Orla was so excited. "Will I be able to talk to my parents?" he asked.

He followed the moonbird's song out of the moon garden

and burst into the palace. "Mother! Father!" he called. He went rushing over to greet them, listening with his bright clear eyes, talking with eloquent hands.

The King and Queen were amazed at the change in their son.

"Orla, where have you been?" they asked him.
Orla did his best to tell them but they could not read his eyes.
They watched the strange and beautiful dance of their son's talking hands and his
silent mouthing. "He seems to be talking to us, but we don't know what he means.
We don't know how to talk back to him," they said to the soothsayer.

"We can learn," said the soothsayer, who had been very quick to pick up the boy's sign language.

"I don't know how!" said the Queen.

"Kings don't talk with their fingers," said the King.

Orla felt so sad.
He so loved his mother
and father and he wanted
to share what he knew.
Just then, the moonbird
flew in through
the window.

"Listen to the song of the bird,"

said the soothsayer. "Then you shall have your answer." The moonbird sang his song.

He sang of the stillness of mountains and the sounds beneath their silence.

He sang of the shining earth as it turns in space.

He sang of the moon and stars and of worlds beyond this world.

"What's it all about?" said the King.

"I can't hear anything," said the Queen.

But Orla heard.

Watching all the while was Moonchild. He hadn't meant to cause so much trouble. What could he do to put it right?

He blew an enormous moon bubble which floated off into space and landed right over the Kingdom. Everyone was wrapped in the moon silence. And what did they hear in this silence?

With their eyes they heard the moonbird's song of the earth.
In their hands they held the moonbird's song of the moon and sun.
In their hearts they felt the moonbird's song of the stars.
They saw and heard and understood as never before.
The King and Queen put their arms out to their son.

"How could we have been so blind? And deaf!"

Orla had something else to show his parents – a pip from the moonfruit in the moon garden. Together they planted the pip in the royal garden.

Now the moontree is a million years old and the moonbird sings from its branches.

Its song is the pictures
in your mind.

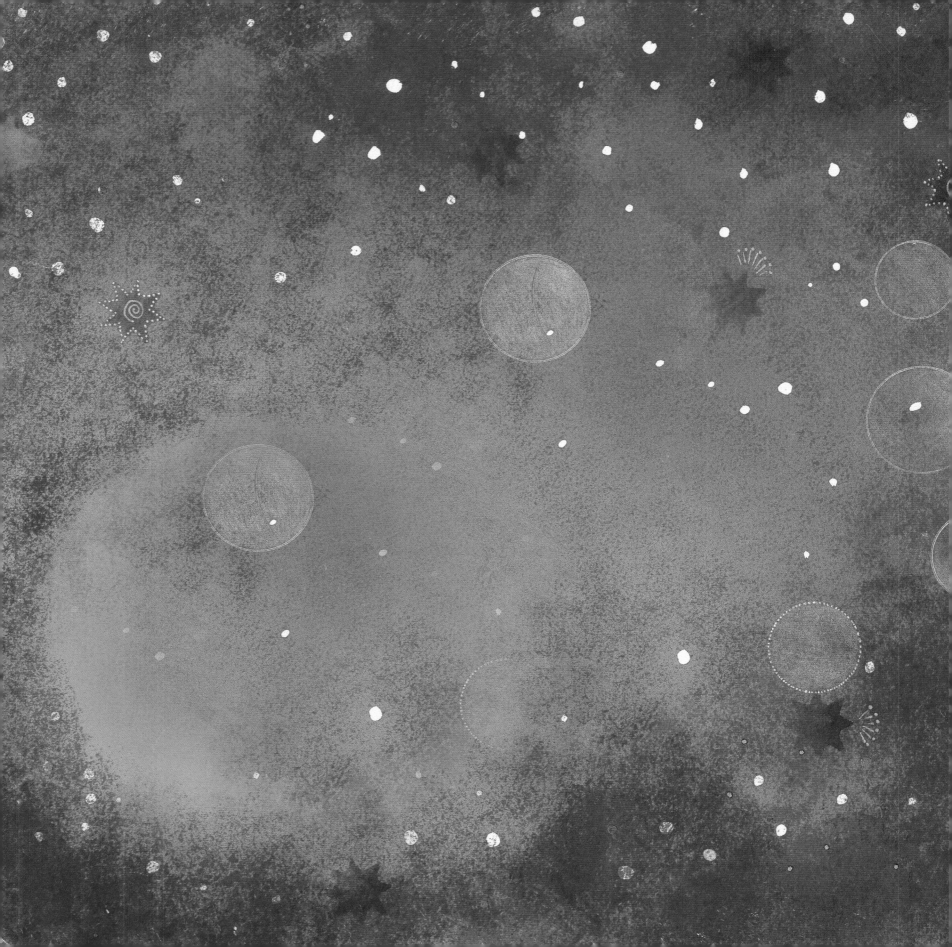